AN ALLOSAURUS ATE
MY UNCLE

Also by Nick Falk and Tony Flowers

With Tony Lowe

SAURUS STREET

An Allosaurus Ate My Uncle

Nick Falk and Tony Flowers

RANDOM HOUSE AUSTRALIA

For my beautiful wife, Carmen. Without your love and support, none of this would have ever happened – Nick Falk

For Charles and Anne, for teaching me to draw and to look for fun in life – Tony Flowers

A Random House book
Published by Random House Australia Pty Ltd
Level 3, 100 Pacific Highway, North Sydney NSW 2060
www.randomhouse.com.au

First published by Random House Australia in 2013

Addresses for companies within the Random House Group can be found at
www.randomhouse.com.au/offices

National Library of Australia
Cataloguing-in-Publication Entry

Author: Falk, Nicholas
Title: An allosaurus ate my uncle / Nick Falk; Tony Flowers, Illustrator
ISBN: 978 1 74275 658 5 (pbk)
Series: Falk, Nicholas. Saurus street; 4
Target Audience: For primary school age
Subjects: Allosaurus – Juvenile fiction
Other Authors/Contributors: Flowers, Tony
Dewey Number: A823.4

Cover and internal illustrations by Tony Flowers
Internal design and typesetting by Anna Warren, Warren Ventures
Printed in Australia by Griffin Press, an accredited ISO AS/NZS 14001:2004 Environmental Management System printer

Random House Australia uses papers that are natural, renewable and recyclable products and made from wood grown in sustainable forests. The logging and manufacturing processes are expected to conform to the environmental regulations of the country of origin.

CHAPTER ONE
My Cousin Walter

'Let me out!'

I push against the door but it won't budge. Walter's **too heavy**. He's leaning against it from the outside.

'Are you going to hand over the money?'

'NO!'

'Then you can stay in there,' says Walter.

1

Why should I hand it over? It's my pocket money. I only get twenty cents a week, and I've been saving up for months. I really want those stickers. And they'll be sold out soon, I just know they will.

I push as hard as I can, but it's no use. The door won't budge. It's so **frustrating**. Why aren't I bigger? If I were as big as Walter he wouldn't DARE lock me in the cupboard. And so what if I'm a girl. I'm much tougher than him. He's just a great big **coward**. That's why he bullies people. He's too scared to try to make friends.

'What's going on up here?'

It's Aunty Gwen. She's coming up the stairs. Walter backs off suddenly

2

and I tumble out of the cupboard and onto the floor.

'We were just playing hide-and-seek,' says Walter, sweet as can be.

Aunty Gwen smiles as I stagger to my feet.

'It's so *lovely* how you two play together,' she says, ruffling my hair. 'Aren't you lucky to have an older cousin who loves you so much.'

Walter smiles *angelically*.

He puts one arm around my shoulder. The other hand goes behind my leg and pinches me painfully on the thigh.

I wince, but I don't squeal. I'm not going to give him the satisfaction.

'Come downstairs,' says Aunty Gwen, trotting off to her bedroom. 'Uncle Colin's just starting on the eggs.'

Walter keeps smiling until Aunty Gwen is out of sight. Then he scowls and twists my arm behind my back. 'Where did you hide it?' he growls.

'I'm not going to tell you,' I say, and stamp on his toes.

'Oooof,' gasps Walter. He lets go of my arm so I give him a shove and race off to my room.

I close my door and check that my pocket money is still there. And it is. All four dollars and forty cents of it. Enough to buy a whole sheet of Limited Edition

4

Super Sparkly
Glow in the Dark
3D Dinosaur
Stickers.

I

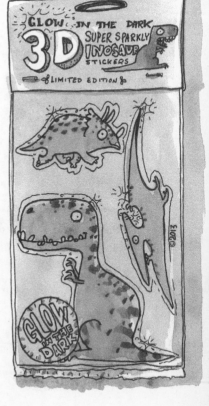

dinosaurs. My
parents are
palaeontologists.
That means they
dig up dinosaur
bones.

And every
time they come back
from a dig they bring me a fossil.
Sometimes it's a stegosaurus spike, or a
brontosaurus jawbone.

Once they gave me a fossilised
triceratops horn. I love that horn. I sleep

with it under my pillow. Especially when I'm staying at my aunt and uncle's house. Walter Attacks can happen at any time.

That's the worst part about my mum and dad being palaeontologists.

Every time they go away I have to stay here. The big old house on Saurus Street.

It's a **brilliant** house. Full of strange little corners and dusty old nooks. But it's got one thing wrong with it. It's got a Walter in it. And I don't like Walters.

'Breakfast time!' shouts Uncle Colin. I put my pocket money back in its **secret** hiding place, pull on my socks and race down the stairs.

7

CHAPTER TWO

Who's in Charge?

Breakfast is always the same at Number 24 Saurus Street. One egg boiled in orange juice. One rasher of bacon with extra hot mustard. And two spoons of cornflakes doused in golden syrup.

'All the food groups together!' says Uncle Colin. 'Sweet, savoury and spicy. Fuel for the day!'

Uncle Colin is tremendously jolly. He has an enormous moustache and always wears a tweed jacket, even when it's forty degrees outside.

Aunty Gwen is as thin as a twig. She also has a moustache, although it's not as big as Uncle Colin's. Aunty Gwen always wears massive hats, even when she's inside. Today she's wearing one shaped like a prancing zebra.

'Now then,' says Uncle Colin, as I silently smear my mustard on the underside of my chair, 'Aunty Gwen and I have an announcement to make.'

'Indeed we do,' simpers Aunty Gwen.

She looks lovingly at Walter. Walter looks lovingly back at her. If there's one thing Walter is very good at, it's pretending to be nice.

'You're twelve years old now, Walter, so it's high time you were given some responsibility.' Uncle Colin shovels another spoonful of syrup into his mouth. 'And so we're going out for the day, and leaving you **IN CHARGE**.'

I freeze, boiled egg halfway to my mouth.

This sounds bad.

'Now,' continues Uncle Colin, 'being **IN CHARGE** is a serious business. It means no mess, no break-ages, and no livestock in the living room. If anything goes wrong, *you* will be held responsible.'

'And you'll need to look after your cousin Susie,' says Aunty Gwen.

'Of course I will,' says Walter, eyes twinkling.

'Make her a nice lunch.'

'Oh yes.'

I quickly stuff the rest of the boiled egg into my mouth. It might be the last thing I eat today.

'And make sure she doesn't get bored.'

'Oh, she won't get bored. I'll make sure of that.' Walter smiles at me. 'I was thinking of having a little treasure hunt.'

'That sounds lovely,' says Aunty Gwen.

No it doesn't. I know what treasure he's after. My pocket money.

Uncle Colin takes off his napkin and straightens his **BOW TIE**. 'Well, Gwennie, we'd better be off. One mustn't be late to a garden party.'

Aunty Gwen leaps up and starts gathering the dishes.

Uncle Colin removes his moustache comb from his top pocket and strides off towards the bathroom. 'And remember, Walter,' he barks mid-stride, 'you can go anywhere in the house, *but no-one's allowed in the attic.*'

12

Walter's grin spreads, showing his **twisty** little teeth. 'Oh, don't worry, Father. We won't go anywhere *near* the attic.'

CHAPTER THREE
Into the Attic

'But your father told you not to!'

'Yes, but Father's not here.'

I try to squirm out of Walter's grip, but he's too strong. He drags me to the top of the stairs. The attic door looms in front of us, black paint peeling off the woodwork.

'Just tell me where you hid your

pocket money and I'll let you go.'

'What do you want it for, anyway?'

'None of your business,' says
Walter, twisting my arm.

I know why he wants it. He's going

to buy more **FIRECRACKERS**. His
spotty friend Spud is coming over. And
they're going to spend the day throwing
firecrackers over Mrs Wilcott's fence.

'Now, are you going
to give me the money
or not?' He bends
my fingers
sbɿɒwʞɔɒd.

It hurts. But I refuse to give in.

'NO!' I shout. 'IT'S *MY* POCKET MONEY!'

'Right,' says Walter, 'then into the attic you go.' He starts opening the door.

The attic is the one place in this house I'm scared of. It's not the old boxes or the moth-eaten shop dummies I don't like. I don't even mind the **cobwebs** and the mice.

It's the door handle.

The old metal door handle.

I heard Uncle Colin talking about it once. About the scientist who used to live here. About how he made a secret door in the attic and did strange experiments up there. And then one day, he **disappeared**. The scientist went up to the attic and was never seen again. And the door disappeared too. All that's left is the door handle, sticking out of the wall.

Sometimes at night I can hear it **rattle**.

Walter opens the door. The attic is dark and musty. There aren't any windows up here. Just a bare light bulb hanging from the roof.

The Daily News 1973

Missing Scientist

X-RAY GLASSES ARE A HOAX

Snoring into the Record Books

Fred Tiblins and cat

'Last chance,' says Walter. He's grinning, but he looks a little **nervous**. Walter's scared of the attic too.

I refuse to speak. He'll never find that pocket money. It's too well hidden.

'Then in you go,' he says. He shoves me into the attic, closes the door and turns the key.

I'm locked in.

CHAPTER FOUR
The Door Handle

I look around the room. I can hear things moving, but that's probably just the mice. There are loads of mice up here. Uncle Colin keeps saying he's going to deal with them, but he never does. I think he quite likes them. 'Mice give an old house character!' That's what he likes to say. And it's true.

There's nothing wrong with mice.

I'm not so sure about the spiders, though. All the boxes are covered in **cobwebs**. Sticky ones. It's impossible to move around up here without getting coated in spiderwebs. And some of the spiders are quite big.

One of the shop dummies is looking at me. It's got black eyes and red lips.

Aunty Gwen used to make dresses, and she owns loads of shop dummies. Only the old ones live up here. The **broken** ones with half their faces

missing. I don't like them much but I refuse to be scared by them. If I get scared that means Walter wins. And Walter is not allowed to win. I grab an old sheet and throw it over the dummy looking at me. Much better.

I can't see the door handle, but I know it's there. Hidden behind Uncle Colin's old office chair. It's **long** and twisty and made of brass. It's the kind of door handle you might find on an old castle in the woods. A castle where a beast might live.

Walter says the old scientist is trapped behind the wall. He says his skin has rotted away, and all that's left are his bones.

HELP!

He says that sometimes, at night, he **scratches** on the wall, waiting for someone to rescue him. But Walter's a lying toerag, so I know that's not true. Still, I don't want to go too close to the handle.

But I have to look at it. I don't know why, I just do. It's more **scary** thinking about it than seeing it. After all, it's just an old metal door handle.

There's a broken broom in the corner. I pick it up and use it to push the office chair to one side. The office chair is on wheels, but they're rusty, so it's hard to move. I give it an extra hard shove and it **squeaks** slowly into the corner.

And there it is.

Sticking out of the blank white wall.

The door handle without a door.

I take a deep breath and force myself to look at it. Because it is only a door handle. It's silly to be scared of it. I wait for it to do something, but it just sits there, doing nothing.

Maybe if I touched it, I'd stop being scared.

'How's it going in there, scaredy-cat?'

Walter's still outside the door. He's hoping I'll start crying. He's such a **beast**.

I take another breath, and start walking towards the wall. I'm eight years old and I'm far too big to be scared by a silly old door handle. I walk right over and stand next to it. I watch it for a while. It still doesn't do anything.

Now all I have to do is touch it.

Here goes.

I lift my hand and slowly move it towards the door handle. And I get closer and closer and closer and . . .

CREAK.

The door handle turns. All on its own.

I yelp and leap backwards.

And that's when the light goes out.

CHAPTER FIVE

Trapped in the Dark

'Walter! Turn on the light!'

The light switch is outside in the passage. Walter turned it off on purpose.

'Awww. Is the ickle baby getting fwightened?'

The door handle starts **rattling**.

Someone's trying to get in. The scientist. It must be the scientist.

I back away as fast as I can. But I can't see. It's pitch-black in here. I trip over a box and **tumble** onto the floor. Cobwebs cover my face and arms.

'PLEASE, WALTER! TURN ON THE LIGHT!'

Walter just laughs. 'I'm . . . coming . . . to *GET* . . . youuu.' He's doing his scary monster voice. Usually it doesn't scare me. But right now everything's scaring me.

'JUST TURN IT ON!'

The door handle stops rattling. And something starts thumping on the wall. Thumping from the other side.

I've got to get out of here.

I need light. I reach into my pocket, looking for my reading torch. It's not there. But I can feel something else. I pull it out. My wishing wand!

'Heugh . . . Heugh . . . Heuuuugh.'

Walter's doing his monster breathing. Stupid Walter. He can't hear the knocking on the wall. If he could, he wouldn't find this so funny.

I shake the wishing wand and the end lights up. Just a little bit. But enough to see in front of me. I walk forward and

YIKES!

A face! Right in front of me! It's a shop dummy. I push it to one side and stagger around it. **THUMP! THUMP! THUMP!** goes the wall.

I hold up my wand and close my eyes. It's worth a try. I turn around three times and make the special swish. Now would be a really great time for my wish to come true. I could use the help.

BLINK. The batteries go flat. So much for my wishing wand.

It's pitch-black again. I reach around me desperately, trying to work out where I am.

And that's when I touch something. Something cold, metal and hard.

It turns in my hand. All the way downwards. Oh no. It's the door handle.

The thumping on the wall stops. I hold my breath. And then a new sound starts. A deep shuddering

rumble.

It's the wall. It's starting to open.

CHAPTER SIX
Something's Coming . . .

I race sbɿɒwʞɔɒd. I don't care about bumping into things. I just need to get away from the wall.

I can hear a grinding sound. There's a faint light spilling into the room, and I can make out the outline of a doorway. And there's something else too. Something large. Something moving.

'WALTER! *WALTER!*'

I reach the attic door and start **banging** against it.

'Is the ickle baby scared of the dark?' says Walter.

'OPEN THE DOOR! OPEN THE DOOR!' I shout.

'Hmmm. I'm feeling peckish. I think I'll go and make myself some toast,' says Walter.

I can hear something breathing now. I can hear **REAL** scary breathing. It sounds deep and ragged. Maybe the scientist turned into a zombie, and he's coming to eat my flesh.

'WAAALTEEER!' I shriek.

Walter cackles to himself. 'See you later,' he says, and wanders off down the stairs.

Something's walking towards me. Its footsteps are slow and heavy. Boxes and shop dummies tumble to the floor as it *LURCHES* across the attic. It's a zombie. Definitely a zombie.

I scrabble around for a weapon. All I can find is a broken coathanger. I clutch it in front of me.

RUMBLE.

The doorway starts closing. I'm going to be stuck in here with the monster. There's no escape now.

The footsteps get closer. And something growls. A deep rasping growl. I hammer against the attic door. But it's locked tight. I'm trapped.

BOOM!

The door closes. I turn around. This is the end. My final moments.

The zombie lurches right up to me. It's just inches away now. And then it leans slowly towards me. Its face pushes right up against my head and . . .

It snuffles my hair.

My heart's beating fast. I reach up a hand. I can feel rough, scratchy skin. And I can feel a nose. A nose with a great big horn on it.

I don't know what it is, but I don't think it's a zombie.

CHAPTER SEVEN
Walter the Wimp

This is one **hungry** monster.

It's been munching its way through the attic for over an hour. It seems especially keen on shop dummies. I can hear it crunching their heads off. Every now and then it nuzzles against my shoulder. Whatever it is, it's awfully friendly.

'Oh, SUUUsie. *SUUUUUsie.*'

Walter's back outside the door. I stay silent, pretending I'm dead. It's about time he got scared for a change. The monster keeps munching. It's finished with the shop dummies and it's started on the boxes. I think it's eating Uncle Colin's stamp collection. Uncle Colin won't be happy about that.

'Are you still in there, scaredy-cat?'

I keep as still as I can. The only sounds that can be heard are chewing and **munching**.

Hopefully Walter thinks I've been eaten. I can hear him listening. He's probably got his ear pressed against the door.

'I hope you're not making a mess,' he says.

Good. He's starting to worry.

36

Walter's **IN CHARGE**, so if I've made a mess, he'll be the one who gets blamed.

CRUNCH!

The monster snaffles up the light bulb.

'What was that?' snaps Walter. 'Are you breaking stuff?'

I keep silent. Walter curses and starts fumbling for the key.

'You better not be breaking stuff. Because if you are I'll –'

CLICK.

'Why isn't the light working?'

Walter opens the door. He's standing in the doorway.

'Susie? *Susie?*' He peers around the attic. 'Where are you, you stupid girl?'

The monster starts ripping something. It sounds like clothing. Clearly it enjoys a varied diet.

Walter curses again and starts searching in the hallway cabinet. He finds a torch and turns it on. 'You better not be hiding from me,' he says. He's trying to sound threatening, but he's **nervous**. I can hear it. He walks tentatively into the room.

'Susie?' he whispers. 'Where are you?' He leaps to the left and shines a torch around a pile of boxes. 'Stop hiding,' he barks, 'you're being silly.'

He's starting to get scared.

The monster makes a loud munching sound.

'Aha!' he says. 'There you are!' Walter swings the torch around and starts walking towards us.

The monster **growls**.

Walter stops in his tracks. He stays frozen for a few seconds, and then forces himself to keep going. 'Stupid girl,' he says, his voice **shaking**. 'Do you really think that's going to scare me?'

I keep as still as I can.

Walter keeps on coming. 'Just you wait until I find you,' he says. 'I'm going to . . . *WHAT'S THAT?*'

Walter's walked straight into the monster. His torch flashes upwards.

39

A huge black face looms in front of him.

'**GRAAAF!**' growls the face.

Walter goes as white as a sheet. And then he starts screaming. He *screams and* screams *and* screams.

And then when all his breath has been screamed out, his eyes roll back in his head, and he collapses in a dead faint on the floor.

The monster nuzzles my cheek. I pick up Walter's torch and shine it on my new friend. It's got four legs, a thick stumpy tail and three long horns on its head.

40

I can't believe it. It's a triceratops.

A real live triceratops.

Who would have thought it? My wishing wand actually works!

CHAPTER EIGHT
The Time Turner

'Where did it come from?' wheezes Walter. He's hunched in the corner, keeping as far away from the triceratops as he can.

'It came through the wall,' I say. 'I thought it was a zombie.'

The triceratops is halfway through chomping down an antique clock.

'How do we get rid of it?' Walter croaks.

'Why on earth would we want to do that?' It's the silliest suggestion I've ever heard.

'Because it's BREAKING stuff!' says Walter.

That is certainly true. The triceratops has chewed up twelve shop dummies, most of the boxes and three

of Uncle Colin's vintage tweed jackets.
Uncle Colin will not be pleased.

'What happened to the door
handle?' says Walter.

I look over at the wall. It's
blank, white and smooth.
You'd never know a door had opened
out of it. But the door handle's fallen
off. It's lying on the floor. It must have
snapped off when I turned it.

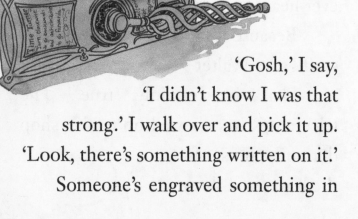

'Gosh,' I say,
'I didn't know I was that
strong.' I walk over and pick it up.
'Look, there's something written on it.'
Someone's engraved something in

tiny spidery writing on the base of the door handle. You wouldn't see it unless you put your nose right up close.

'What does it say?' says Walter.

I start reading.

'TIME TURNER
Turn clockwise to go backwards and anticlockwise to go forwards.
Batteries not required.'

That explains it! The scientist must have invented a Time Turner and used it to travel to a different time. That's why he **disappeared**. Maybe he went to the Cretaceous period to live

with the dinosaurs. Or maybe he went into the future. I'd love to go into the future. I bet the toys would be brilliant.

'Well, let's use it!' says Walter. 'Let's send the dinosaur back!'

He's staring bug-eyed as the triceratops munches noisily on Aunty Gwen's wedding dress. And who can blame it. It's pink and fluffy and looks like candy floss.

Walter's looking less and less pleased about being left **IN CHARGE**.

He reaches out gingerly to rescue the dress. But he's too late. The triceratops gulps it down and starts hunting for dessert. It pushes past Walter and **tramples** down the stairs.

'Oh no,' whines Walter. We hurry out of the attic and race down after it.

We find it in Aunty Gwen's bedroom. Walter takes one look at it and **freezes** solid.

'No . . . please, not the tutu.'

He looks like he's about to faint again. I elbow my way past him. Oh dear. The triceratops is  polishing off Aunty Gwen's ballet outfit. The one she wore to the Under

10s state finals in 1979. Apparently it's priceless.

'Please,' begs Walter, 'you've got to help me.' He looks distinctly unwell. 'I'm going to get annihilated.'

I don't know what that means, but it sounds unpleasant. And possibly **fatal**. Walter may be beastly, but that doesn't mean I want him dead.

The triceratops belches loudly. That tutu obviously hit the spot.

'All right,' I say. 'I think I have a plan.'

Walter looks pathetically grateful.

'But I have to warn you,' I say, 'you're not going to like it.'

CHAPTER NINE
Hats the Plan

'But why?' whines Walter. 'Why the hats?'

I'm using Aunty Gwen's hats to make a trail up the attic stairs.

'Because General Galantus clearly likes to eat tulle.'

Walter stares at me blankly.

'Tulle,' I say. 'It's the netting stuff

they make tutus and wedding dresses out of. Aunty Gwen uses it to make her hats.'

She uses lots of it too. Especially on her Sydney Harbour hat. The whole Opera House is made of tulle. I place it gently on the top step. 'General Galantus will enjoy that one.'

'General Galantus?' says Walter.

'It's his name,' I say. 'I think it suits him.'

My triceratops may be **greedy**, but he has a commanding presence. I watch him fondly as he scoffs Aunty Gwen's African savannah hat. Lions and rhinos don't stand a chance against a triceratops.

'I can't bear to look,' says Walter.

50

General Galantus
is halfway up the steps.

'Now remember,' I say, 'I'm only helping you do this on the *sworn promise* that you stop bullying me.'

Walter nods dully.

'*And* you give me half your weekly pocket money.'

Walter sneers.

'Unless you'd like me to guide General Galantus to Uncle Colin's study?' I start moving the hats.

'No, don't,' says Walter. 'I agree to everything.'

He's such a **WIMP**.

He's too scared to go near my triceratops. That's why he needs my help. General Galantus reaches the top of the stairs. I start laying a hat trail into the attic. I think we're going to have just enough. Aunty Gwen is going to be seriously short of hatwear from now on.

'Another thing,' I say, 'we're

only sending General Galantus home because you're **IN CHARGE** and you'll get blamed for the mess. As soon as you're NOT **IN CHARGE**, we're bringing him back. Agreed?'

I've always wanted a dinosaur and I'm not giving him up just because he likes eating hats.

'Fine. Whatever,' says Walter. 'Let's just get on with it.'

We're halfway across the attic. I've got one hat left.

'Right,' I say, 'time to see if this thing works.'

CHAPTER TEN
Stampede

'Do you want to do it?' I hold out the door handle to Walter, but he shakes his head and backs away.

'You did it the first time,' he says. 'Maybe it only works for girls.'

He's such a baby.

I walk over to the wall. I can't see a hole where the door handle goes, so

I just hold it against the wall. And the door handle **sinks** right in, as if the wall's made of playdough. I let go of it, and it just sticks. Now that's clever.

Okay then. Clockwise to go backwards. That's what it says on the door handle. And that means turning it to the right. Although it doesn't really matter where I send General Galantus. I'll be bringing him back as soon as Uncle Colin and Aunty Gwen get home.

Uncle Colin has always wanted a pet, and triceratops make spectacular pets. They keep the grass short and **munch** up all the rubbish. It's even better than recycling!

I turn the door handle to the right and step back. Almost immediately the wall starts *shuddering* open. The doorway is about three metres high and reaches almost to the roof. Beyond it is a dark stone tunnel. It looks a bit **scary**.

I throw the last hat into the tunnel and step back. It's a multicoloured affair with picnicking teddy bears on top of it. Tulle galore. I'm sure General Galantus will go for it.

But he doesn't. He just stands there, staring into the tunnel. And then *he* backs away too. Now that's really strange.

What on earth has a triceratops got to be scared of?

'What's that sound?' says Walter.

Something's rumbling. It starts off quietly, and then gets louder and louder. It sounds a bit like an . . .

Everything in the attic starts shaking.

'What's going on?' squeaks Walter, backing towards the attic door. He's getting ready to run.

'I'm not sure,' I say. 'It sounds like something's coming.'

'Yes,' says Walter, 'but *what*?'

It doesn't take us long to find out.

The rumbling gets **louder** and

louder until it's

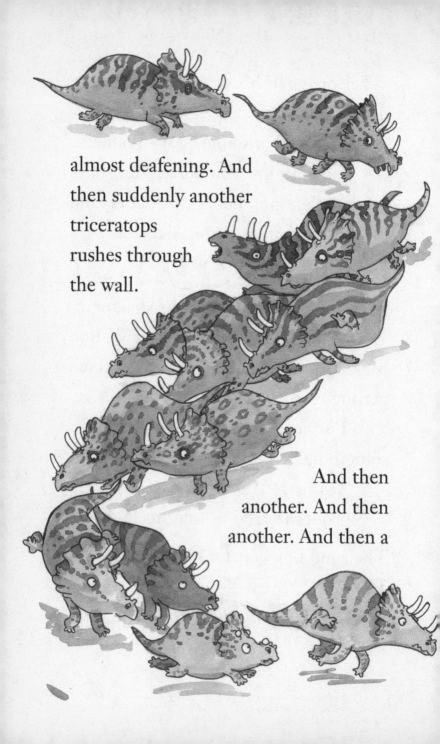

almost deafening. And
then suddenly another
triceratops
rushes through
the wall.

And then
another. And then
another. And then a

whole herd of triceratops barges into the room.

'It's a STAMPEDE!' wails Walter.

He tries to escape but he can't. There are too many triceratops, and they're all rushing down the stairs.

It's a dinosaur traffic jam.

'It looks like they're running from something,' I say. They do seem to be in a terrible hurry. 'I wonder what it is?'

'THAT!' screams Walter.

I look up. There's something else coming through the wall. Something considerably larger than a triceratops. And considerably more terrifying. It

opens its mouth and **roars**.

Its mouth contains more teeth than I can count. And maths is my best subject.

I don't think this is a dinosaur that
wants to make friends.

CHAPTER ELEVEN
Spud

Walter and I race down the stairs. I'm **squeezed** between a baby triceratops and a fat one with a stripe on its bottom. I can't see where Walter is, but I can hear him wailing. Wherever he is, he's not having fun.

I reach the bottom of the stairs. There are triceratops everywhere. I spot three of them barging through

Aunty Gwen's bedroom, two of them **crunching** through Uncle Colin's study and four of them **SMASHING** their way through the bathroom. Not a single piece of furniture has survived.

ROAAAAAR!

The mighty meat eater has reached the bottom of the stairs. I think it's an allosaurus. You can tell by its row upon row of razor-sharp teeth. Mum gave me a poster of one once. I thought the razor-sharp teeth were brilliant at the time. Now I'm not so sure.

The allosaurus snaps its jaws at a triceratops and then turns its eyes on us. Walter's just appeared next to me.

He's covered in something brown. I think it's triceratops poo. 'We're going to die!' he squeals, gasping for air. A triceratops rushes past, stamping on his toes as it goes. Walter's face turns purple. The colour combination doesn't suit him at all.

The allosaurus starts lumbering towards us. It's so **tall** its head is scraping the ceiling. No wonder General Galantus was thumping on the wall to come in. This is one theropod you'd never invite over for tea.

We spin around and sprint out the front door. And almost run straight into Walter's friend Spud.

'You must be psychic,' says Spud. 'I was just about to knock.'

He's standing on the front step, dressed in orange shorts and an oversized baseball cap. He's holding a bag of firecrackers.

'Did you forget I was coming over?' he says.

SMASH!

The front door goes flying. An enormous triceratops comes bundling through.

'Blimey O'Reilly,' says Spud. 'Where did you get him from?'

CRUNCH!

The rest of the herd follows swiftly after.

'Crikey,' says Spud. 'Did you get them on discount or something?'

KAPOW!

The doorframe explodes into splinters. The allosaurus pokes its head through and roars.

'Whoa,' says Spud. 'Now that one you should keep on a leash.'

Walter screams and gallops across the garden. Spud and I race after him.

'If I'd known we'd be running, I'd have worn my trainers,' says Spud.

We follow the herd down the road and into the woods. The triceratops are setting a healthy pace, but the allosaurus is gaining.

'The Time Turner!' squeals Walter. 'Use the Time Turner!'

'Use what?' says Spud.

I look down. The door handle! I've still got it! It must have snapped off in my hand when I turned it.

'What do I do with it?' I shout back at Walter.

'Just stick it in a tree!' he yells.

I suppose it's worth a try. I press it into an enormous eucalypt. And it **Si**n**kS** into the bark, just like it did in the attic wall. But it won't turn. I push as hard as I can but it's stuck.

'Let me do it,' snaps Walter, shoving me out of the way.

He grabs the door handle and pushes down on it. He strains until his face goes red, but it won't budge.

I look back. The allosaurus is almost on to us. In five seconds time we'll be breakfast.

'Maybe if we all do it together,' I say.

'Do what?' says Spud, looking

be·fuddled

The allosaurus growls, showing us its teeth.

'QUICKLY!' squeals Walter. He grabs Spud's hand and puts it on the door handle. Then we put our hands on top and push. And it turns. Just a tiny bit, but it turns.

'It's not enough,' wails Walter.

We spin around. The allosaurus lowers its snout. We're about to get munched.

'MUUUMMYYYY!' howls Walter, closing his eyes.

RUMBLE goes the tree. I look behind me. It's working! A doorway's opening in the tree trunk!

'MOVE!' I shout at Walter, shoving him to the left. Spud and I dive to the right.

SNAP!

The allosaurus charges straight between us and disappears through the doorway. I pull the door handle off the tree and the doorway closes with a

BANG!

We did it. It's gone.

We all flop to the ground, gasping for breath.

'Do you know what?' croaks Walter. 'I hate dinosaurs.'

CHAPTER TWELVE
Goodbye Saurus Street!

'So you're saying the dinosaur went into the tree?' asks Spud.

'Yes!' I say. It's about the hundredth time I've tried to explain it to him.

'But I still don't get it,' says Spud. 'It wouldn't fit inside the trunk.'

We're walking back through the woods. General Galantus is plodding

along next to
me. The other
triceratops are
following. I knew
he was a leader. I named him well.

'Look,' says Walter. 'Helicopters.'

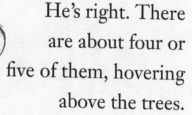 He's right. There
are about four or
five of them, hovering
above the trees.

'Someone must have spotted the
dinosaurs,' I say. 'Maybe they phoned
the police.'

The helicopters are buzzing
everywhere. Walter looks ill. He was
hoping to keep this quiet.

'This is *your* fault,' he snaps, 'so *you*
get to do the explaining.'

'Uh-uh-uh,' I say, shaking my head.

'You're **IN CHARGE**, remember?'

Walter grinds his teeth.

We reach the edge of the forest and peer up the road. It's a . Fences flattened, cars crushed, trailers trampled. Walter's going to be in serious trouble.

'I've got it,' says Spud. 'We leave the beasties here, stroll out of the forest and act casual.'

Walter and I look at each other. It's the first good idea he's had.

I turn to General Galantus. '*Stay*,' I say, and put a finger on his snout.

General Galantus grumpfles, and then he sits. The other triceratops follow suit.

'I didn't know you could talk dinosaur,' says Spud. He looks impressed. 'Hey, Wazza, your little cousin's kinda cool.'

'Shut up,' says Walter.

We stroll out of the forest. The damage is even worse than we thought. Trees smashed, power lines destroyed, walls knocked down. A couple of houses are even **on fire**.

'Surely we didn't do all this,' gasps Walter. It looks like someone's dropped

a bomb on Saurus Street.

Suddenly we hear a wail.

'OH! Oh oh oh!'

Someone rushes down the road towards us. It's Aunty Gwen. She's in a complete state. Her clothes are torn, her glasses are broken and her hair looks **mangled**. She's not even wearing a hat.

'Where *were* you?' she gasps. She rushes right up to us and raises her arms.

I cringe. Are we about to get whacked? No. We're about to get

hugged. And wow, what a hug. Aunty Gwen puts her arms around all three of us and just keeps on hugging.

'We thought we'd lost you,' she weeps.

'Er,' says Walter, 'no. No. We're all right.' He looks a bit **BAMBOOZLED**. 'I thought you and Dad went to a garden party?' he says.

'A *party*?' exclaims Aunty Gwen. She looks at him as if he's gone mad. 'There aren't any *parties*, Walter. I've been in **hiding**. Just like everyone else.'

Walter gives me a look. Something very strange is going on.

'What have you been hiding from?' says Spud.

'The *monster*, Sebastian, *the monster*.
What else would I be hiding from? It's
already eaten half the street.'

'Eaten?' I say.

Aunty Gwen looks pained. 'Mrs
Wilcott,' she says, 'gobbled up in her
bathrobe. Little Jack, snaffled on the
swings and . . . and . . . and –' she puts a
hand on Walter's shoulder '– your poor
father, Walter, eaten in his finest tweed.
Right in the middle
of breakfast.' She
bursts into
floods of
tears.

We all stand there, feeling rather **awkward**. And that's when something occurs to me.

'Aunty, how long has the monster been here?'

'Over a week now,' she sobs. 'Oh, the horrible beast. It just appeared out of nowhere, like a nightmare.' She starts wailing again.

I pull Walter and Spud to one side. The helicopters keep on **buzzing** overhead.

'I think I know what's happening,' I whisper.

'Well, I'm glad one of us does,' says Spud. 'I haven't got a clue.'

'It's the dinosaur,' I say, 'the meat eater. I think we sent it back to *here*.'

'What are you talking about?' snaps Walter. 'We sent it *from* here, not *to* here.'

'No,' I say, 'you don't understand. Remember the door handle in the tree? Remember how it only turned a little bit?'

'Yes,' says Walter.

'Well, maybe it only sends things back as far as it gets turned.'

Walter stares at me with distaste. 'What are you talking about?' he snips.

I roll my eyes. 'We only turned it a little bit, so we only sent the dinosaur back in time a little bit. To Saurus Street. About a week ago. *That's* what's been eating up the street. *That's* the monster Aunty Gwen's talking about. *That's* what ate your dad.' Whoops. That was a bit insensitive. But Walter doesn't appear to notice.

'So then we're going to have to go back to last week and stop it?' asks Walter.

'Precisely,' I say. 'And then nobody gets eaten.'

Spud stares at us, a **baffled** expression on his face. 'What are you two blathering on about?' he says.

I turn back to my aunt. 'Aunty Gwen,' I say, 'we have to go.'

'What?' She looks **horrified**. 'But I've only just found you.'

'I know', I say, 'but, er . . . we've made a bit of a mess, and I think we better clean it up.'

Aunty Gwen stares at me. And then her eyes widen. 'No,' she gasps, 'do you mean you are responsible for . . .'

'Yes,' I say, as we back away towards the woods. 'I'm really sorry.'

Aunty Gwen looks appalled, her mouth gaping. 'But, but, but . . .'

'But it was Walter's fault!' I add. 'After all, he was the one **IN CHARGE!**'

Walter boots me in the shins.

CHAPTER THIRTEEN

Romans!

'I can't believe it,' says Walter. 'You **destroyed** Saurus Street.'

We're walking back to the woods. Walter's marching in front of us.

'Me?' I say. 'I didn't do it! It's not my fault.'

'Of course it's your fault,' he spits. 'You're the one who let the dinosaur out of the attic.'

'But you're the one who *locked* me in the attic,' I say. 'I wouldn't have been up there if it wasn't for you.'

'So what?' says Walter, spinning around. 'You're the one who turned the door handle.'

He jabs a finger at me. 'Because of you, my dad got eaten.'

That is so **unfair**.

I never meant for Uncle Colin to get eaten.

'But he won't be eaten,' I say, 'not when we go back to last week. He'll be alive again in a minute.'

'Not if you have anything to do with it,' snaps Walter. He snatches the door handle from my hand. 'This time

I'll turn it. Otherwise you'll just muck it up again.'

We've made it back to the triceratops. They're busily chewing up the undergrowth. General Galantus lowers his head and I scratch him on the chin. He grunkles with satisfaction.

'I think you're being mean,' I say.

'You're an eight-year-old girl,' snaps Walter. 'Nobody cares what you think.' He starts inspecting the trees, peering closely at their trunks.

'What are you doing?' says Spud.

'Making sure we pick the right tree,' says Walter. 'She must have stuck it in the wrong one last time. That's why the door handle didn't turn properly.'

Spud stares at the trees. 'They all look pretty much the same to me.'

'That's because you're thick,' says Walter. He stops in front of an **enormous** ghost gum. 'This one should do,' he says. He sticks the door handle into the trunk and turns it. This time it turns without any problem. 'See?' he says. 'Easy.'

He stands back and waits for the doorway to open.

'You turned it too far,' I say.

'No I didn't,' says Walter.

'You did,' I say. 'It only turned a few centimetres last time. You just turned it halfway.'

Walter ignores me. The doorway starts **grinding** open. We all peer around it. On the other side we can see more woodland. It looks pretty much the same as where we are now.

'See?' says Walter. 'Saurus Street. Let's go.' He starts moving forward and then pauses. 'After you,' he says, standing aside.

I roll my eyes and walk through the doorway. General Galantus walks next to me, the other triceratops following behind.

We come out in another forest. It looks a lot like the woods we came

from. And we can hear talking.

'See?' says Walter, stepping through the doorway. 'People. Didn't I tell you? We've come back to last week.'

We start walking forward. Walter keeps me and Spud in front of him, just in case we see the allosaurus. We come to the edge of the forest. But there's no Saurus Street. Just open grassland leading down to the sea. We've come

back to a time before Saurus Street even existed.

'Last week, eh?' I say.

Walter fires a **dirty** look at me.

'Check it out,' says Spud. 'Boats.' He points out towards the water.

And he's right. There are four enormous wooden boats anchored near the beach. They've got lines of oars sticking out of their sides.

'Those are Roman longboats,' says Spud.

'Roman what?' says Walter.

'Longboats,' says Spud. 'That's what they went invading in.'

'What are you talking about?' says Walter. 'This is Australia. The Romans didn't invade Australia.'

'**BARBARIANS**!' A shout goes up. Suddenly there are men all around us. Men wearing white cloaks, metal helmets and carrying swords.

'ROMANS!' shrieks Walter. He turns around to run away, but it's no use. There are more men behind us. Rough hands grab us by the arms and start dragging us towards the beach.

'Brilliant,' says Spud. 'I love the Romans.'

89

CHAPTER FOURTEEN
Hanging Around

'I will ask you again. Where is your village?'

The Roman centurion is marching up and down below us. He's wearing a golden breastplate and he's got a huge red feather sticking out of his helmet.

I think he looks rather **silly**.

'We don't come from a village,' says

Spud. 'We come from Saurus Street.'

Walter tries to kick him. But he can't reach. It's not that easy kicking someone when you're tied up upside down over a pit of **sharpened** spikes.

Walter's hanging in the middle with Spud and me on either side. The triceratops are tied up too. They're not looking too pleased about it. General Galantus is keeping quiet but the one with the stripe on its bottom is making an awful racket.

'Which one of you is in charge?' asks the Roman centurion.

'Him,' I say, pointing at Walter.

'Shut up,' says Walter.

The Roman centurion points his sword at Walter. 'I will give you until sundown,' he says, 'and if you do not tell me what I want to know, I will kill each of you in turn. Starting with that one.' He points his sword at Spud. Spud gives him the thumbs up.

The Roman centurion marches off, leaving us **dangling** over the spikes.

'This is terrible,' whines Walter. 'What are we going to do?'

'This is amazing,' says Spud, grinning. 'Who would have thought it? Romans in Australia. Mrs Simms never

taught us about this in history class.'

I start **swinging** on my rope.

'What are you doing?' says Walter.

'Shush,' I say.

I learnt this in gymnastics. If you can swing hard enough on a rope while you're upside down, you can swing yourself upright and grab the rope with your hands.

'Stop it,' squeaks Walter, 'you're going to knock into me. You're going to make me fall.'

I use my upper body to build up momentum and then I **scissor** myself upwards. And it works! I grab hold of the rope with my hands and start shimmying upwards.

'Wow,' says Spud, 'you're like Catwoman or something.'

I reach the top of the rope, hold onto the branch and untie myself. Then I somersault down to the ground.

'That was **awesome**,' says Spud.

I tiptoe to the branch and start lowering Walter.

'Careful!' he yelps. 'Watch out for the **spikes**!'

I lower him to just above the pit, then pull him towards me and untie him. Then I lower Spud.

Walter looks around him fearfully. 'Quick,' he says, 'let's get out of here.'

'We can't,' I say. 'The Romans are camped all around us.' I start freeing

94

the triceratops. They're really heavy, so Spud has to help me.

'Then how are we going to escape?' whines Walter. 'They'll catch us and kill us. And I don't want to be **KILLED**.'

'We're going to have to fight them,' I say.

'Fight them?' says Walter. 'But they're Romans. They've got swords. And we're just children.'

'Yes,' I say, 'but we've got something they haven't got.'

'What?' says Walter.

I smile at him. 'Dinosaurs.'

CHAPTER FIFTEEN
Charge!

We reach the top of the hill. The Romans are waiting for us, swords in hand. They're all holding **enormous** curved shields. When they see us, they group together and hold their shields in front of them.

'That's called the tortoise formation,' says Spud. 'The Romans invented that.'

'Right,' I say, 'I'll take the middle. Spud, you take the right. Walter, you bring up the rear.'

I'm sitting on General Galantus's back, holding on to his horns. It didn't take long to persuade Spud to do the same. He's riding Stripy Bum.

Walter's at the back, riding the baby triceratops. He was too scared to ride a big one. 'What if I fall off?' he kept saying.

The Romans start **banging** their swords on their shields.

'Wahoo!' cries Spud. 'This is brilliant. Time travel really brings history to life.'

I raise my hand.

'Battle formation!' I shout. The triceratops line up and lower their horns.

'Ready!' The triceratops start rumbling.

'CHARGE!'

The triceratops .

Spud whoops. Walter whimpers. And away we go!

We charge down the hill towards the Romans. General Galantus races out in front, the rest of the herd following close behind. The sound of their feet **thunders** all around us.

'WAIT FOR IT!' shouts the Roman centurion. 'WAIT FOR IT!'

General Galantus lets out a mighty roar.

'RUN AWAY!'

The Romans start scattering. They drop their shields and swords and sprint towards the boats.

'RETREAT! RETREAT!' screams the Roman centurion.

We chase them onto the beach and watch as they swim out to the boats and start rowing away as fast as they can.

'HOORAH!' shouts Spud.

Suddenly I hear a snorting noise behind me. I turn around. And here comes Walter, trotting up on his baby triceratops.

'I told you the Romans didn't invade Australia,' he says.

And I can't believe it. He's actually smiling!

'Are you all right?'
I say.

'Never better,'
he says. 'I think I
could get used to this.'
He pats the triceratops on
the neck. The triceratops grunts at
him. Walter's heavier than he looks.

'Well, what do we do now?' says
Spud.

'We go home,' I say. 'We've got
a street to save and an uncle at risk of
becoming dinosaur food.'

There's a GIGANTIC
rock on the beach. I jump down off
General Galantus and walk over to it.
Walter follows me.

'So have you got a plan?' he says.

And he hands me the door handle. Just like that. Without a single rude comment. I take the door handle and hold it against the rock. It **S**i**nk**S right in.

'I do have a plan,' I say.

I get a good grip on the door handle and turn it anticlockwise, making sure I turn it just enough. The rock starts **rumbling** open. We hurry back over to our triceratops and mount up.

'Are you ready?' I say.

'Yup,' says Walter. Spud gives me the thumbs up.

'Then let's go back to the future.'

CHAPTER SIXTEEN

Hello Saurus Street!

We charge out of the rock and onto the beach. It's a **hot** sunny day, and the beach is packed. Children run screaming from us, adults squeal like babies and seagulls squawk with terror.

'Excuse me,' I say to a hairy man in tight blue speedos, 'but what day is it today?'

'Saturday,' squeaks the man, clutching his boogie board for safety.

'What date is it?'

'Um . . . February the third.' He looks around for help, but everyone's steering well clear of our dinosaurs.

'And would you mind telling me what year it is?'

'2013,' mumbles the man, clearly deciding I'm **bonkers**. He backs away from General Galantus and stumbles over a sandcastle.

'Thank you very much,' I say.

I kick General Galantus into a trot and head towards the road. Walter and Spud are riding beside me. Cars swerve to get out of our way. Two of them **crash** into each other, horns

104

screeching, and another one swerves into a lamppost.

'Are you sure we've come to the right time?' asks Walter, sounding a bit worried.

'Yes, it's the perfect time. Two months BD.'

'BD?'

'Before Dinosaurs.'

Spud looks confused. 'But the dinosaurs lived *ages* ago. How can this be before dinosaurs?'

'Before *our* dinosaurs,' I say. 'This

is two months before Walter locked me in the attic.'

'Ah,' says Spud, looking utterly befuddled.

We start heading up Saurus Street. The summer school fete is in full swing and the park is packed with families. The crowds take one look at my triceratops army and start racing for the woods. It's complete and total

m^{a}y$_h$em.

'Are you sure this is a good idea?' asks Walter.

'It's an excellent idea,' I answer. I've just spotted Miss Potts, my horrible class teacher. She's just run straight into a tree. Spud spots her too, and bursts out laughing. Nobody likes Miss Potts.

'But aren't we going to get into **trouble**?' asks Walter.

'No,' I say, 'we won't get into any trouble at all.'

'Why not?' asks Walter.

'Because by the time we've finished, none of this will have ever happened.'

We reach Number 24 Saurus Street and turn into the gate. General Galantus doesn't quite fit and takes most of the gate with him.

'Hello!' I shout as we trample into

the house. Aunty Gwen and Uncle Colin are just sitting down to morning tea.

'Ah. There you are!' barks Uncle Colin from the kitchen. 'How are the festivities going?'

'Super,' I say, as General Galantus barges through the hallway and heads for the stairs.

'Well, make sure you don't make any mess,' calls Uncle Colin. 'Gwennie's just done the vacuuming.'

CRUNCH!

Spud thunders through the front door on Stripy Bum. 'Mornin' Mr and Mrs G!' he hollers as he goes. Walter scurries behind him on Baby, looking rather sheepish. We start clomping up the stairs.

'My goodness, you three are making a racket,' shouts Uncle Colin.

'You sound like a pack of dinosaurs. Did you remember to take your shoes off?'

'Yes!' I shout, as General Galantus puts his foot through a floorboard.

'So what's the plan?' whispers Walter when we're safely upstairs.

'We're going to get rid of that allosaurus,' I whisper back.

'What?' asks Walter, going rather

109

pale. 'Do you mean the gigantic one with razor-sharp teeth?'

'Yes, that one,' I say.

We reach the top of the stairs and **stomp** into the attic.

'So what happens when we get rid of the allosaurus?' asks Walter.

I shrug. 'No dinosaurs,' I say. 'The only reason the triceratops ran through the wall is because the allosaurus chased them. If we get rid of the allosaurus, we get rid of the triceratops too. None of this will have ever happened.'

'I see,' says Walter. 'But I thought you always wanted your own dinosaur?'

'I did,' I say, 'but I think one day with a dinosaur is enough. They're rather a handful.'

Walter smiles.

'And anyway,' I say, climbing down off General Galantus, 'I'm keeping the door handle, so there's nothing to stop him coming round for tea.'

I give General Galantus a tickle on the chin. He rubs his snout against my shoulder.

'So let me get this straight,' says Spud. 'We're about to take on a gigantic **BLOODTHIRSTY** prehistoric killer.'

'That's right,' I say.

Spud turns to Walter and grins. 'I love coming over to your house,' he says.

CHAPTER SEVENTEEN
Taking on the Allosaurus

I put the door handle in the wall and turn it to the right. All the way **downwards**. The doorway grinds open with a shuddering rumble.

I take the door handle and climb onto General Galantus's back.

'Let's do it,' I say.

We start walking down the stone tunnel. It looks like we're in some sort of cave. There are stalactites dangling from the ceiling and bats flying overhead. Very big bats.

BOOM!

The doorway closes behind us. And just like that we're in darkness.

'SQUAWK!' goes something high above us.

'Walter,' whispers Spud, as we slowly make our way through the darkness. 'If you get eaten, can I have your computer?'

'No,' says Walter.

'I promise I'll look after it.'

'I said no,' says Walter.

Suddenly there's light in front of us. It's the cave entrance. We come out onto a grassy plain. There are GIANT ferns and purple fruit trees all around us.

General Galantus grunkles in the back of his throat.

'This must be where the triceratops live,' I say. 'It's beautiful.'

And it is. If I were a giant plant-eating reptile, I'd live here too.

Something starts growling. Something in front of us. It's a growl so deep it makes the ground SHAKE.

'And that must be the reason the triceratops left,' says Walter, blood draining from his face.

I gently nudge General Galantus forward. He doesn't like it, but he keeps moving. We push our way through ferns and vines and giant creepers, and come out on a rocky plain at the edge of a cliff.

And there it is. The allosaurus. It's about fifty metres in front of us, and it's eating something. It looks like a stegosaurus. It's using one giant foot to hold the stegosaurus in place, and it's ripping off great chunks of it with its RAZOR-SHARP teeth.

'So,' whispers Walter, 'what's the plan?'

'Same plan we used for the Romans,' I say.

'We just run at it?' asks Walter.

'Yes,' I say, 'but we do it together. We're six dinosaurs against one. If we do it together, it'll run away.'

'Righty-o,' says Walter. 'Well, if it's all the same to you, I think I'll take the rear again.' He turns Baby around and quickly trots to the back of the herd.

I take a deep breath. Here goes nothing.

'BATTLE FORMATION!'
I shout. The triceratops line up next to me. The allosaurus lifts its head and stares at us. It doesn't look very worried.

'READY!'

The allosaurus curls its lip and **growls**. Spud gives me the thumbs up.

'CHARGE!' I shout. And we're

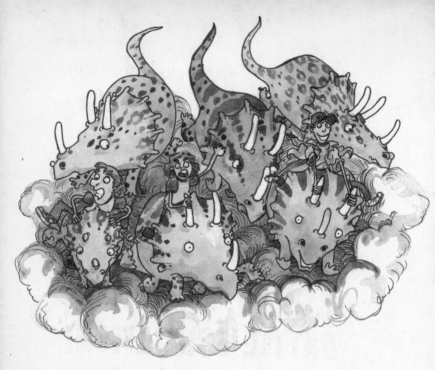

off. The triceratops race forward, horns down.

'YAH!' shouts Spud, waving his hands in the air.

The triceratops give an answering roar. But the allosaurus doesn't budge.

And we get closer and closer and closer. And just as we're about to leap over the

dead stegosaurus, the allosaurus darts forward, roaring and **snapping** its teeth. The triceratops scatter. Spud tries to keep Stripy Bum from running, but it's no use. Stripy Bum is too strong.

And I'm left there, on my own, face to face with a killer.

CHAPTER EIGHTEEN
Over the Edge

The allosaurus edges forward, saliva **DRIPPING** from its teeth. I can feel General Galantus shaking, but he stands his ground.

'Run away!' shouts Spud.

But we won't. Not now. We can defeat this monster, I know we can.

The allosaurus lowers its head and stares at me, waiting. I get a good grip on General Galantus's crest, take a deep breath, and urge him forward.

'Let's get him,' I whisper.

General Galantus paws the ground with his feet. And then he *races* forward, horns lowered. We're going to jab the allosaurus in the chest. But at the last moment the allosaurus dodges to the right and slams its head into General Galantus's side. General Galantus tumbles to the floor and I'm sent flying.

OOF!

I hit the ground and roll over and over until I slam into a rock.

The allosaurus steps forward. It lowers its head. It's going to eat General Galantus! But then it lifts its eyes and stares at me. It knows I'm the one in charge. It steps over General Galantus and starts **STOMPING** towards me. I'm about to get munched. I shut my eyes tight and wait for it to be over.

'Hey!' someone shouts. 'Get away from my cousin!'

I open my eyes. And I can't believe it. Walter's riding to my rescue, on Baby.

'You horrible great bully,' says Walter. 'Pick on someone your own size.'

He plucks a purple fruit from a tree and flings it at the allosaurus.

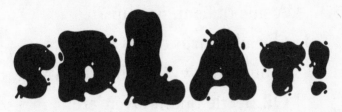

It hits the allosaurus on the forehead.

The angry dinosaur turns around and thunders towards him.

'Ah!' shrieks Walter. He hadn't planned for that. 'Now let's be reasonable here,' he says. 'I'm sure we can discuss this.'

Baby triceratops starts backing away, straight towards the cliff.

'Perhaps I could arrange for a sausage delivery? I know an excellent butcher.'

Baby's back legs scrape over the cliff.

'A side of ham, perhaps?'

The allosaurus opens its jaws.

'Muuummyyyy...' wheezes Walter.

'Oi! Beetle brain! Over 'ere!'

The allosaurus turns.

Something explodes in front of its face. It's Spud, armed with firecrackers. He's tied his t-shirt around his head and painted mud on his cheeks, like war paint. He's painted some on Stripy Bum too. 'Time to feel the pain!' shouts Spud. He charges forward, flinging firecrackers as he goes.

SLAM!

Stripy Bum hits the allosaurus smack in the chest and sends it tumbling backwards. But Spud's not holding on, and as Stripy Bum slides to a halt, Spud slips off his back. And follows the allosaurus, straight over the edge of the cliff.

'NO!' I shout.

I don't think. I just act. I race to the edge of the cliff and throw myself forward. And I just manage to catch Spud's hand. But hang on! What about me? I forgot to hold on!

SNATCH!

Something latches on to my wrist. I jerk to a stop in mid-air, Spud dangling below me. I feel like I'm being torn in two. I look up. And there's Walter, one hand holding a tree root, the other hand holding me.

Walter smiles. 'Next time,' he says, 'let's just stay at home and play snakes and ladders.'

CHAPTER NINETEEN
Home Again

General Galantus comes with us all the way back through the cave.

'Goodbye,' I say, and kiss him gently on the nose. He grumpfles softly and leans his head against my shoulder.

'Come on,' says Walter, 'let's go home.' He puts the door handle in the wall and *turns* it all the way to the

left. The doorway starts grinding open.

I give General Galantus one last **cuddle**. A good long cuddle for a very special friend. And then I follow Walter and Spud through the doorway. It closes with a **BOOM** behind us.

The attic is neat and tidy. All the boxes are in the right place, and all the shop dummies have their heads on. Even the one with black eyes and red lips.

'I wonder what day this is?' says Walter.

'Hello! We're home!' It's Aunty Gwen, calling up the stairs.

'I think it's today,' I say.

'What?' says Walter.

'Today. The day you were left **IN CHARGE**. I think it's this afternoon already.'

Walter stares at me for a moment, utterly puzzled. And then his eyes widen. 'Oh no!' he says. 'We're in the attic! We're not allowed up here!'

We run to the attic door, pull it open and race down the stairs, two at a time. We reach the landing just as Uncle Colin strides into view.

'Ah,' says Uncle Colin, 'there you are.' He gives us a suspicious look. 'You

130

weren't mucking around in the attic, were you?'

Walter and I shake our heads as quickly as we can. 'No,' we both say.

'Good,' says Uncle Colin. 'Well, the house looks in good order. Nothing broken, I see. So, did you get up to any

mischief?'

Walter, Spud and I look at each other. I stifle a grin.

'Nah,' says Spud, 'we had a quiet one.'

'Pity,' says Uncle Colin. 'I used to get up to all kinds of mischief when I was left in charge.'

He takes out his moustache comb and marches off to the bathroom. 'Kids today,' he mutters, 'they've got no sense of adventure.'

CHAPTER TWENTY
One Last Time

I shake the triceratops horn, but there's nothing there. My pocket money's **gone**. I can't believe it. How did Walter find it? How did he know the horn was hollow?

My bedroom door opens and Walter creeps in. He looks **sheepish**.

'You took my pocket money,' I say.

Walter looks at his feet. 'I did,' he says, 'I admit it.'

He puts his hand in his pocket, takes out my pocket money and tips it onto the bed. And it's all there. All four dollars and forty cents.

'Why did you take it then?' I say.

'Because I didn't want you spoiling your surprise.'

He reaches into his bag and pulls something out. It's the stickers. The stickers I've been saving up for. I can't **believe** it. He bought them for me, using his own money.

'Now don't think this means I like you,' he says, handing me the stickers. 'You're still a pain in the backside, and

you still can't touch any of my stuff,
but –'

'But what?'

'But I suppose it's okay having you
around. Sometimes.' He gives me a
gentle shove and walks over to the door.
When he gets there he stops and turns
around. 'It's a shame we lost that door
handle, isn't it?'

'Yes,' I say.

'Probably for the best, though,' he
says. 'I'm not sure I'd survive another
day like yesterday.'

'No,' I say, 'neither would I.'

I try and stop myself from smiling.
But it's difficult. Fibbing makes my lips

twitch.

Finally Walter walks out of the room.

'Phew,' I say. I relax my face and uncross my fingers. You're allowed to fib if you keep your fingers crossed. I reach under the bed and pull out the door handle. He'd never have found it anyway. It was hidden behind my velociraptor skull.

It's not like I plan to go time travelling every day. I just want to give General Galantus one last hug. It'll be easy. Up to the attic, through the door, into the cave, hug the dinosaur and home again.

What could possibly go wrong?

SAURUS STREET

Saurus Street is just like any other street . . . except for the dinosaurs.

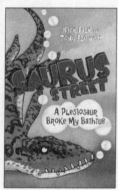

Collect them all!

Watch out for
Billy is a Dragon
by Nick Falk
and Tony Flowers
coming in March 2014